MW00963230

Hayden's Glasses

Written by Janelle Booth & Illustrated by Vanessa Harder

There is a boy we call Bobayden.
(Actually, his name is Hayden.)

He's a really awesome kid to know.

He has lots of stories and tricks to show.

Upon his face there sits a pair of cool blue glasses that he likes to wear.

The glasses help his eyes to see

the world around him,
clear as can be.

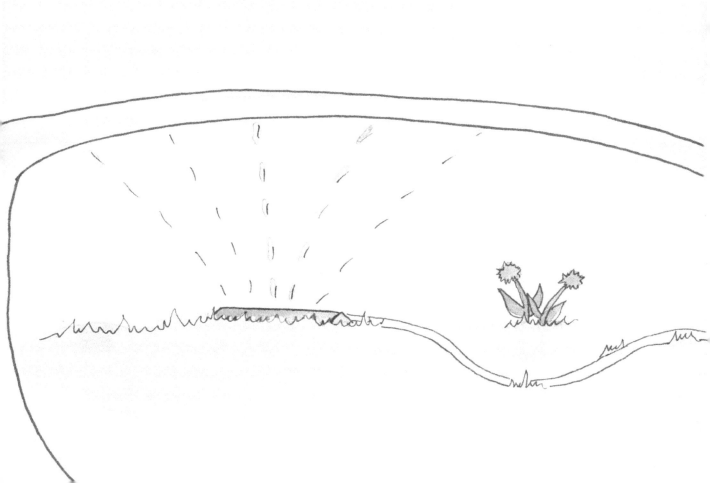

Somehow every single day
those silly glasses hide away.

Where are your glasses?

his mom will shout.

You need them on when we go out!

"I had them on my face,
but then...
I turned and they were
gone again!"

They come off when
big tears tumble.

They hide away when
daddy wants to rumble.

The baby grabs them
off his face.

They vanish when Super H
saves the human race!

While he's in the bath,
they avoid the splash.

And sometimes when playing
they end up in a crash.

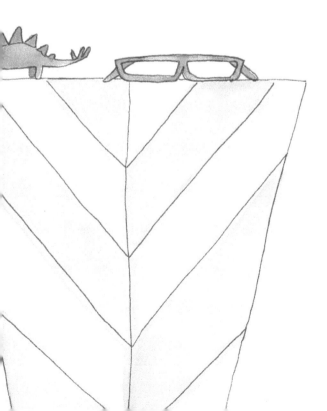

When story time is over
and Hayden's ready for sleep
he takes off his glasses
so he can count sheep.

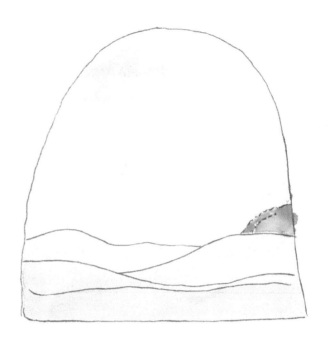

They are sure to sit still
by the edge of his bed

until morning light comes and they return to his head.

The End

For Hayden. Thank you for making me a mama
and giving me endless things to write about <3 - J. B.

Dedicated to Travis. - V.H.

First Edition Published in 2019
by JB via IngramSpark
Text @2019 by Janelle Booth
Illustrations @2019 by Vanessa Harder

All rights reserved.
No part of this book may be reproduced in any form
without written permission from the publisher.

Book design by Lakeview Times
Typeset in Macshandwriting.
The illustrations in this book were rendered in ink and watercolour.

ISBN 978-1-9991457-1-2
10 9 8 7 6 5 4 3 2 1

#haydensglasses

CPSIA information can be obtained
at www.ICGtesting.com
Printed in the USA
LVHW020953240719
625084LV00001B/1/P